Alycia Oppenheim has a bachelor's degree from the University of South Florida and a master's degree in Shakespeare Studies from the Shakespeare Institute in England. Passionate about social change, Alycia strives to make a difference in the world. Apart from working at her full-time job, she is currently a student at the University of Kent earning a second master's degree in English and American Literature.

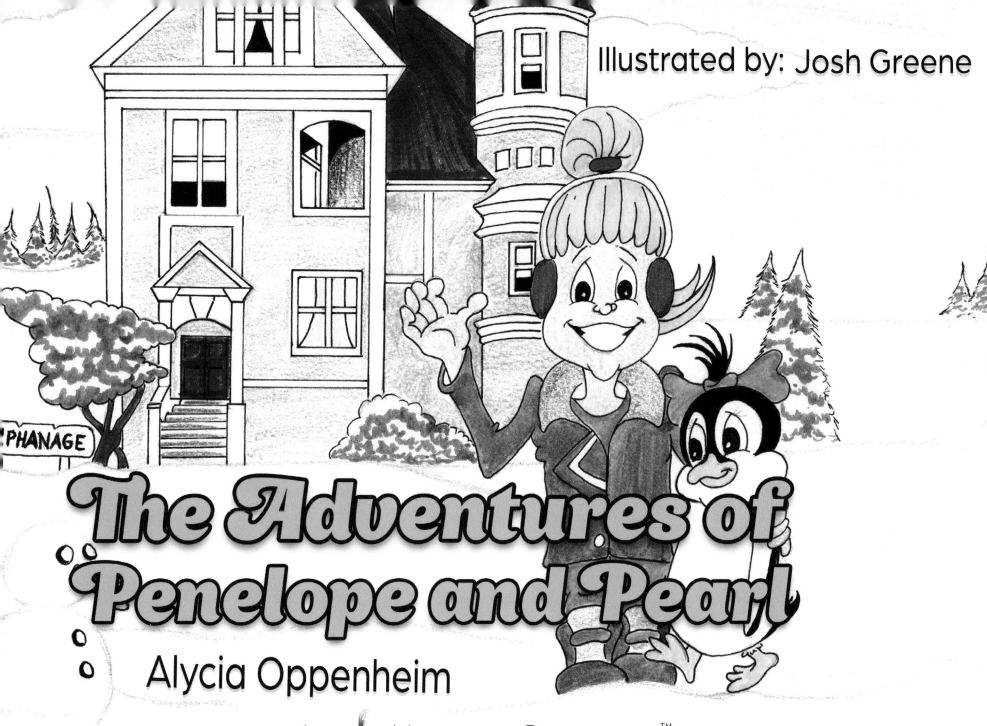

Illustrated by: Josh Greene

PHANAGE

The Adventures of Penelope and Pearl

Alycia Oppenheim

AUSTIN MACAULEY PUBLISHERS™
LONDON * CAMBRIDGE * NEW YORK * SHARJAH

Ordering Information
Quantity sales: Special discounts are available on quantity purchases by corporations, associations, and others. For details, contact the publisher at the address below.

Publisher's Cataloging-in-Publication data
Oppenheim, **Alycia**
The Adventures of Penelope and Pearl

ISBN 9781649793614 (Paperback)
ISBN 9781649793621 (ePub e-book)

Library of Congress Control Number: 2021900452

www.austinmacauley.com/us

First Published (2021)
Austin Macauley Publishers LLC
40 Wall Street, 33rd Floor, Suite 3302
New York, NY 10005
USA

mail-usa@austinmacauley.com
+1 (646) 5125767

To Landon, Madyson, Olivia and Lilyan.

Doda loves you.

There are so many people who inspired me to finish the first book of *The Adventures of Penelope and Pearl* – to all of you, thank you. To Nanny Shirley, my inspiration for Mrs. Pearson, thank you for the love you showered me with in my earliest years. To Adina, a special thank you for your outlook and fresh ideas for this book and the future of Penelope and Pearl. And, last but certainly not least, a very special thank you to Lief, who first brought Penelope to life.

Glossary:

Adoption: When one person or two people make the choice to become mommies and daddies to children that do not have their own mommies and daddies.

Orphanage: A home where children who do not have parents can live.

Penelope always wanted to have a friend. She was a late hatcher, so she came out much smaller than all of the other penguins. She was always left out of all of the penguin activities because she was tiny. All the other penguins her age bullied her, so she would just sit on top of the glaciers to watch and dream of what fun she would have if she only had someone to play with.

One day, while lying on the ice, daydreaming with her eyes closed, Penelope heard her father yelling to her from far away. She didn't understand why her father sounded so far off because she was just below their home. However, when she opened her eyes, she realized that the ice had moved and she was miles into the sea. Penelope was still too small and too furry to swim and didn't know what to do. She had no way to get home and her father had no way to get to her because of the egg he was keeping warm on land.

Penelope became very sad. She didn't know where she would end up, or if she would ever see her parents again. As the sun went down, Penelope tried to close her eyes and dream. It was only in her dreams that she could find happiness.

Not so far away there was a little girl named
Pearl, sitting by the water, wishing for a family.
At 8 years old, Pearl was already one of the
smartest students in her class. She liked school
but didn't like being called a teacher's pet. None
of the other kids ate lunch with her or played
with her at recess.

Pearl would tell the people at the orphanage that
she didn't mind, but it was there, as she sat by
the water all alone, that she could be honest.
Pearl so wished she could have a friend.

Pearl looked up into the sky and saw the evening star. It was then that she wished for a friend so she wouldn't be so lonely. She believed that her parents were coming for her and a friend would give her something to smile about until they did. All alone, Pearl walked back to the orphanage to go to sleep, still thinking of her wish and her hopes that it would come true.

The next morning, as Pearl sat near the water, she saw something coming towards her. To her little eyes, it looked like an animal, but why would there be an animal just floating on a piece of ice? As the piece of ice got closer, the animal started to take shape. Pearl saw that it was a baby penguin coming near her and that it looked like it was lost. When it got close enough, Pearl pulled it onto the ice near her and watched the little baby penguin sleep.

When Penelope opened her eyes, she saw this weird animal in front of her and jumped off of the ice and hid behind it! "Who are you?" said Penelope to the weird creature.

"You can talk? But you're a penguin! Penguins can't talk!" responded Pearl in a scared voice.

"All penguins can talk. We are just picky about who we talk to."

"Well, my name is Pearl. What is yours?"

"My name is Penelope, and I am an Emperor Penguin. What kind of penguin are you?"

Pearl giggled and said, "I'm not a penguin, Penelope. I'm just a little girl. What are you doing all the way over here? Are you lost?"

Penelope began to cry and explained the whole story to Pearl. She told her that she had been daydreaming on the ice near her home when the ice broke off, and she couldn't get back on land.

"Why didn't you just swim back? Penguins can swim, can't they?" asked Pearl, with curiosity.

"Yes, penguins can swim," replied Penelope, with tears in her eyes, "but I am too little and would sink if I got in the water, so I couldn't swim home."

"I'm all alone too. My parents went on a vacation to heaven and left me at an orphanage."

"What's an orphanage?"

"It's a place filled with people who will take care of you and love you until they find you a family. Hey! I'm sure they will let you stay there too. You don't have a family either."

"Do you really think so?" asked Penelope. "Do you want to play a game with me before we go? I've never had someone to play games with."
"I'd love to play a game! I always get left out at the orphanage."

Penelope and Pearl played together for the rest of the day until it was time to go inside the orphanage. They played with a ball, and Penelope showed Pearl how she could walk on top of the ball. Pearl showed Penelope how she could jump rope. They stayed out until the moon rose up into the sky, forgetting about the time and all of their troubles. Both just had so much fun, now that they finally found a friend.

One day, when Penelope and Pearl arrived home at the orphanage and were getting ready for bed, Pearl noticed Penelope looking out the window.

"What's wrong, Penelope? Aren't you happy to be here with me?" asked Pearl.

"Of course. You are the best friend that I've ever had. But sometimes, I miss my parents."

"I miss my parents too," replied Pearl as she reached into her hair and pulled out her bow. "When I was little, before my mommy went to heaven, she gave me my scarf and this pretty bow. When I get sad, I hold them to my heart, think of her, and it always makes me feel better." With a smile on her face, Pearl placed the bow in Penelope's hair.

17

"I want you to have this bow, Penelope, because you're the best friend I've ever had too, and I hope that when you're feeling sad, this bow will make you feel better like it always makes me feel better."

The girls hugged and got ready for bed. As they drifted off to sleep, with Penelope with a bow in her hair, both girls had smiles on their faces, for they knew no matter what, they would never be alone again.

Two weeks passed during which Penelope and
Pearl spent their
days playing games together. They sat
on the grass and rolled the ball. Pearl
pretended to be a penguin like Penelope, and
they waddled. The girls had found something
they both had been searching for, a friend.
Each day was a new adventure; a new game
or place for them to share.

On one cold day, Pearl and Penelope decided to go to the pond that had frozen over in order to ice-skate and play winter games. When they arrived, Penelope decided to teach her new best friend the perfect way to slide. Even with the cold weather, the girls stayed out until the sun began to set all the while laughing and smiling.

When they got home, Pearl began to think and felt like something was missing. Pearl really wanted a mommy and daddy.

When the sun went down, Pearl would carry Penelope up the stairs of the orphanage, and they snuggled in bed and made wishes to the stars in the sky. Penelope wished that she would never have to leave Pearl. Pearl wished for a mommy and daddy to come adopt her and Penelope.

One day the orphanage lady, Mrs. Pearson, told Pearl some exciting news. Two people who wanted to adopt a little girl were coming to visit her the next day. Pearl was so excited, so she ran upstairs as fast as she could and told Penelope the news. She also told Penelope that they had to be on their most perfect behavior or they wouldn't get adopted. Pearl thought to herself how scared she was, so she sat next to Penelope and told her best friend all of her fears.

"What if they don't like me?" said Pearl.
"They will love you, just like I do!" Penelope said back with a smile on her face. "I believe with my whole penguin heart that this is going to be our family!"

The next morning, Pearl woke up feeling nervous but very excited. Since the two people weren't coming until late in the day, Pearl had plenty of time to play with Penelope.

They chose to walk to the water and spend time drawing pictures and angels in the snow. A few hours passed, and they knew it was time to go home.

When they got home, it wasn't very long until there was a knock on the door. She put on her prettiest outfit and her lucky scarf.

Mrs. Pearson put Pearl into the living room area and went to open the door. Penelope hid behind the couch. Two people walked into the room with Mrs. Pearson. She said, "Pearl, I would like you to meet Mr. and Mrs. Cherish."

27

"Hello, Mr. and Mrs. Cherish," whispered Pearl to the beautiful man and woman who sat beside her.
"Hello, Pearl. My name is Rebecca and this is Joshua.
That is a very beautiful scarf you have on," said Mrs. Cherish with a beautiful, bright smile on her face.
"Thank you. My mommy gave it to me before she went away."

"Well, it is lovely. What games do you like to play?" asked Joshua.
"I love to push the ball around and pretend to be animals and play with dolls," said Pearl happily.
"Do you have a favorite animal?" Rebecca asked.
Pearl giggled and said, "Oh yes, my favorite animal is a penguin."
Rebecca and Joshua smiled at Pearl. They looked at each other and nodded their heads. "Pearl," said Rebecca, "how would you like to come live with us?"

28

Pearl smiled, and jumped up and down, and said, "Really??? Oh, that would be wonderful! But, can my best friend come too?"
"Well, who is your best friend, Pearl? Can we meet her?" asked Joshua.

Pearl looked over to the corner of the couch behind where Mr. and Mrs. Cherish were sitting and said, "It's okay, Penelope, you can come out now."
After a few seconds, little Penelope waddled out from behind the couch and introduced herself. "Hi! My name is Penelope, and I would like to come home with you too."

Rebecca laughed and said, "Well, I think we can find space for two little girls. What do you think, Joshua?"

Joshua smiled and said with big wide-open arms, "Welcome to the family, Pearl and Penelope Cherish."

Pearl raced upstairs with Penelope in her arms to pack up all of the possessions that she had. All of her dreams had finally come true. All of her wishes for a friend and for parents were granted. When she got downstairs, she looked at the people who were now her new parents. "Well girls," Joshua said. "Are you ready? This is the start to some awfully big adventures."

LOOK FOR THE NEXT ADVENTURE OF PENELOPE AND PEARL

30

TO BE CONTINUED

CPSIA information can be obtained at www.ICGtesting.com
Printed in the USA
LVIW011902230221
679750LV00005B/155